THE BIG GAME

TOM DMYTRIW

AuthorHouse™
1663 Liberty Drive
Bloomington, IN 47403
www.authorhouse.com
Phone: 833-262-8899

Because of the dynamic nature of the Internet, any web addresses or links contained in this book may have changed since publication and may no longer be valid. The views expressed in this work are solely those of the author and do not necessarily reflect the views of the publisher, and the publisher hereby disclaims any responsibility for them.

Any people depicted in stock imagery provided by Getty Images are models, and such images are being used for illustrative purposes only.
Certain stock imagery © Getty Images.

This book is printed on acid-free paper.

ISBN: 979-8-8230-0096-3 (sc)
ISBN: 979-8-8230-0097-0 (e)

Print information available on the last page.

Published by AuthorHouse 03/08/2023

authorHOUSE®

THE BIG GAME

I had just woken up, and it was a beautiful Fall morning in New Jersey!!

It was cool and crisp and the trees were simply beautiful – the golds, reds, and oranges of the maples were incredibly breathtaking, as were the blooming chestnut trees now loaded with chestnuts inside the spiked cocoons.

Best of all, it was only a few days away from when my beloved Philadelphia Eagles would be playing the LA Rams in the "game of the century!" Both teams were undefeated and had made mincemeat of all their previous opponents.

All week, my friends and I had discussed the game, and made plans to watch the game at one of my friend's homes.......my studies were going well, Fall was in full bloom, the Big Game was right around the corner...... LIFE COULD NOT BE BETTER!

As I hustled down to breakfast and got ready for school, my mom said, "Tommy, don't forget your Youth Fellowship is going to the Galloping Hills Rest Home on Sunday for their annual Christmas party."

I froze solid at this reminder!!

Holy Cow, how could I have forgotten that my church youth group's annual visit to the rest home was the day of the Big Game!

My world had come crashing down!

"But Mom," I pleaded, "Sunday is the Eagles game and me and the guys have made plans to watch it at Nicky's house!"

My mother, bent over the stove in her terry-cloth robe, making some more bacon, never looked up but simply said, "Tommy, you made a promise to attend this party and this is much more important than a football game."

"But Ma,"…………..and that's as far as I got since the school bus was navigating our leaf-strewn road to pick up the kids on Charlotte Street to get us to school on time.

Well, the rest of the week seemed endless and was very tough as I had to tell my friends I would not be watching the Big Game with them – who wants to waste a Sunday with a bunch of old-timers!

Well, Sunday finally came around, and even Maxie, my family's beloved Westie, could not make me smile.

Wow, I couldn't believe I was going to miss this game!

After our normal routine of church and going to the town diner for lunch, we got home and Mom told me to start getting ready for the ride to the rest home…………boy, was I in one FOUL mood!

Mom and Dad drove me to church where our Youth Director, Mr. Elliott, had rented a small bus to bring us to the Galloping Hills Rest Home.

Mom's parting words were, "Tommy, have a good time and enjoy yourself," at which I responded, very bitterly, "easy for you say to say, I'm missing the BIG Game!"

Strangely, I thought, both my parents simply smiled, and said, "trust us, you will feel different when you get home."

Well, I went to the back of the mini-bus and sat with one of my friends, who was not a sports fan, and tried to not think about the game, which was near kick-off.........boy, I hope the Eagles win, I whispered to myself.

It was about an hour's ride to Galloping Hills, and I have to admit, the scenery was in full autumnal glory – the maples were resplendent in their orange, red, and gold hues.

Mr. Elliott reminded us that going to the rest home's Christmas Party was an annual custom for many, many years and that the old folks there had prepared an outstanding dinner for us along with caroling, and other holiday festivities.

Still very upset with missing the BIG Game, I started to mellow out but as we got closer to Galloping Hills I started to think that Jesus would be happy if I embraced the party and brought some cheer to the residents.

As soon as we got to Galloping Hill, we were met by several of the residents who reminded me of my grandparents.

Now, my parents had me later in life so I did not have a lot of memories with my grandparents, but what little I had, the warm feelings I had for them were reignited instantly by meeting these wonderful people.

The residents were overjoyed to meet with us, and many had tears in their eyes, including me, as we were so lovingly received by them. As we entered the facility, the Christmas decorations were simply beautiful and some more feelings of nostalgia wafted over me.

It just dawned on me that the Eagles game had started…I wondered what the score was.

We were going to be singing Christmas carols later in the afternoon but first we were treated to a wonderful hot dog and all the trimmings dinner…….boy, was I hungry!

Strangely, I was in a great mood, and also very happy, as my group started to attack the delicious food and started to bond with the residents.

As we chatted with the residents, and started to know them better, time seemed to fly and before we knew it, the meal was over and we were free to walk around the home and meet some of the residents who were unable to attend the luncheon.

I still had that warm glow running through my body when I realized that is was just about halftime of the Big Game.

Well, as I walked about, I came to the room of an older man who had been unable to attend the lunch.

He saw me peeking into his room, smiled, and invited me in……………uh-oh, I thought, what did I get myself into?

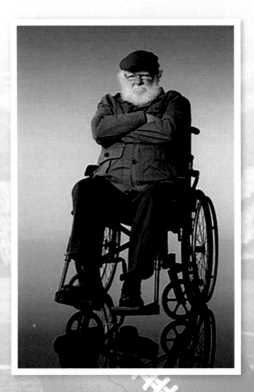

He was sitting in a wheelchair and said, "Hello, my name is Joe, and I'm very sorry I was not able to have dinner with you, but as you can see, I don't walk very well," he joked.

I laughed and introduced myself and when I saw his happy face, and his wonderful voice, I soon forgot he was in a wheelchair and I began to feel a little ashamed of myself that I had been so upset about coming here.

He said to please call him "Old Joe," as he was known in the home, and he told me about his life, which I found fascinating.

Old Joe had fought in World War 1 and he had many pictures on the wall from his days in the Army, and his civilian life.

One of his favorites was a picture of himself in the band uniform of his hometown – he looked so handsome and young.

In speaking with him, I was reminded of my Grandfather and thought of how much I loved and missed him, and the rest of my grandparents.

It was getting dark outside, but I didn't notice it, and we continued to talk and talk until it was time to leave – which I didn't want to do.

Old Joe and I hugged each other and tears were in both of our eyes and he told me, "I wish my son was able to visit me, but you sure remind me of him!"

I felt so happy that I brought some happiness to Old Joe and told him that I would try to stop by and see him again real soon.

We went to the home's lobby, said our good-byes to our new friends, and started to board the bus to go home…………..what a great day this was and I thanked God for the opportunity He gave me to spread some joy and fellowship to folks who needed it so badly!

When we got home, my parents were waiting and Dad said, "do you know who won the Big Game?" I sheepishly looked at my dad and replied, "I forgot all about it!"

Printed in the United States
by Baker & Taylor Publisher Services